Forbidden Delight

Book 3

Phoenix Skyy

Mind Flow Publishing & Production LLC

Additional copies of this book and others are available by mail.

Mind Flow Publishing & Production LLC

PO Box 48768 Cumberland, North Carolina 28331-8768

by visiting the website listed below.

Check the website for pricing.

www.mindflowpublishingproduction.com

Cover Design by RJ Creatives

Formatting by Carlette Whitlock

Mind Flow Publishing & Production LLC

ISBN PAPERBACK 978-1-951271-79-4

ISBN EBOOK 978-1-951271-80-0

FORBIDDEN DELIGHT

Contents

Dedication

A special dedication to all of my family and my friends.

Thank you for being by my side.

Thank you to God for guiding my path

PROLOGUE

NETTE

If you had told me just a few months ago, I would be dating the most elite man in the city and CEO of MidnightZ, a panther-owned business. I would've laughed at your face. Growing up in poverty, I hated the rich with a fiery passion. Sure, hate is a potent word — and not something most people think sweet and wholesome Nette is capable of. But when you watch your loved ones suffer. While others thrive with more than enough to not only survive but help at least a hundred other families thrive too... You grow bitter. This bitterness was blooming deep in my stomach with each good deed I helped my sweet mother with. It bloomed when I met Noah, a man I fell for despite my best efforts not to. A man who embodied everything I fought against.

Yet I still loved him. I still do. And I always will. Noah Kahan is the panther shifter of my dreams — a dream I never knew I had. Or that was possible. With my toes dripping with the waters of luxury, I have my foot in the door to make even more changes in my home community and even within this strange pack itself.

The MidnightZ Gala is an absurd event, and in between strange hunting rituals and political discussion, I do my best to track down my birth family. Only with each hello and subtle introduction, they pretend not to hear. They walk away. I know it's to be expected, but I at least thought they'd be civil in a public setting. Not that some activities my eyes witnessed could be considered civil at all. *And they consider wolf shifters to be inhumane!* I long to point out their hypocrisy.

I also long for the announcement that I am his mate. A forbidden poor girl, an abandoned panther, mating with the heir to the Midnight Shadows Pack? It's scandalous. After the hell his family has put me through — put both of us through — I need this moment.

Only when the time comes, I see my birth father shouting. Calling out a strange pack law - a law that will allow him to fight whoever he so desires in order to solve a dispute. And this fight? It can result in death with no punishment from pack members. When he invokes this law to Noah's father, my world stops. Apparently, Noah's world keeps going because before I know it, he is volunteering to take his father's place.

All I can think is — how dare the Universe take away the best thing I even get to fully have it?

When Noah requests seven days for preparations, I know what I must do. And I have seven days to do it.

Chapter One

Noah

"Noah, we should talk about this. Right? I mean, I think this is something we should talk about..."

"I'll still declare you as my mate soon. We will have a traditional mating ceremony. I promise." My voice sounds a thousand miles away. The hallway leading to my bedroom is closing in on me, but I can't let myself take notice. Not now, Noah. Breathe dammit. You are stronger than this.

Ordinarily I wouldn't sacrifice myself for my father. I spent so much of my life being sacrificed by him for his agenda. My time. My childhood. My innocence. It's a wonder a girl as soft and kind as Nette reached through my walls. Of course, her hips and delicate hands played a huge role in that — in the beginning. Now, I really do want to call her my mate. I want it to be official. We are in the eye of the storm. Everyone knows about us. My parents accepted this fate, our fate. And our relationship bloomed from sex and survived secrets and threats no one should ever endure. Least of all my sweet Nette.

Sucking in a deep breath, I push away my fear and replace it with what I learned is a close relative. Both emotions make you sweat, increase your heart rate, and cause your breathing to grow ragged. "Fuck me," I command.

Nette's jaw drops. "Noah. We need —"

"Do I look like I am worried about that pathetic old man? No offense. I mean, he is technically your father." Sharp. Pointed. My words catch me by surprise, but she's not buying it. "Nette. Our pack is insane. I told you this. It's not like your little makeshift pack back home. But I am safe. I am not worried about this. So, you shouldn't be either."

"If you say so..."

"I do." I bite my lip, reaching my hand over to let loose her curls. "And since we are doing what I say, I believe I already told you what to do."

"Say it again," she says, knees trembling as she leans up against me. Her tongue grazing my ear as she whispers, "It sounded good."

"Fuck. Me."

Obediently, she channels her shifter strength and slams me against the mattress. It's rare to see this dominant side of Nette, and I crave it. Before topping me, she locates the switch to my "little sex chamber" as she calls it. Ordinarily, I would be annoyed by the title, but it's Nette.

It's Nette — words that should hold so much power. Power to override any silly pack law, but it doesn't, and I hate it. I push away the fears of our future, or rather what could be the end of our future and embrace Nette's delicate frame. She pulls away, and looks down at me, as if she is taking in every inch of my body. Memorizing it. The unspoken words — *what if we can't make this work? I want to remember you forever.*

Slipping off her dress, bra, and then her panties, she walks over to the chamber. Her ass has a little bounce to it. She reaches for the handcuffs, whips, and to my surprise a vibrating butt plug. She doesn't think... she plans on using this on herself, right?

I am kinky, but most of my 'toys' have always been to pleasure others.

"Turn around," Nette commands, without so much as a single pause or falter in her tone. "And put these hand-cuffs on."

I do.

She calls out for Alexa to play passionate music, the soundtrack to our romance.

I hear her reach for the lube in my nightstand.

"Take off your pants."

I do. Fuck, I'm liking this role reversal more than I thought I ever could, but I am nervous too. I've never been submissive to someone else in the bedroom. Fuck, I'm always the one in charge in almost any scenario. It's Nette, though... and I trust her with my life.

Nette towers over me, I feel the tip of her nipples graze against my back as she takes my cock in her lubed hands. Stroking me slowly, I tense when I feel a cold vibrating sensation against my ass. "Shh," she whispers. I consider using my safe word, but fuck it feels so good. I almost come from the sensation of that alone. It's new — and sure, I know where the male g-spot is located, but it was never something I had been willing to explore.

I moan when the plug is in. God, how am I gonna keep from coming? Nette lets go of my cock before sliding under me.

"Come inside." She winks.

"Fuck." I bit my lip. And I do. I enter her body, drowning my fears in her. The vibration enhancing every sensation - the way her warmth grips around me. My claws curl into my own skin, as I try to keep myself from spilling into her. Biting, licking, and nibbling every inch of her smooth skin, I reach my handcuffed arms over her head and lock us together. Her hips rise to meet me in a wild rhythm, and I feel her clenching even tighter around my dick.

Her whimpers surround me, drowning out the music. She is my music. My life. And no matter what happens, she *is* my mate. Fuck these outdated pack laws.

I feel her body quake as the vibration in my ass continues to heighten everything so much more than I ever knew was possible.

"Noah," she cries out, her orgasm welcoming me to my own.

I fall over, spasming longer after her body and breathing has settled. "We're definitely adding that to our routine."

"Routine? What am I? A workout regimen?" She giggles, slapping my arm gently, and purring as she stumbles into my body.

"It's gonna work out, Nette," I murmur into her hair, unsure if she can hear me. Exhaustion sweeps over me, and I feel my eyes close before I can tell her I love her. I need her to know... know who she is. What she is.

Because she is Nette — and she is my everything and whatever faces us, I can survive it because she is by my side. In the darkness of my mind as dreams lay claim to my mind, I see our future together — a wedding, children, a true power couple. I am consumed with hope and love even when I drift to another consciousness.

"Thanks for the wild night." She winks, but I can see the flirtatious attitude doesn't meet her eyes. In fact, her entire demeanor has been different since the sun rose. Why? I thought it was just the stress of everything catching up to her, but doesn't she feel the same hope I do? That seem deep knowing...

"Nette," I say. We sit parked in front of her home. I was going to invite her to move in with me yesterday. I had an entire romantic plan to "propose" but that was before I realized I might be dead in a week. So much has changed in such a short time. "Don't worry about all that silly pack stuff, okay? Soon enough it'll be just me and you, and we may have some shit to deal with and some dangerous people, but we'll get through it."

"Mhm," she responds dismissively, her eyes averted. It's as if she can't wait to get out of the car and run through the door to her home. Her home... I sigh. My home was going to be her home if shit hadn't hit the fan.

"I love you, Nette." I never say it first. It feels awkward on my tongue, leaving me vulnerable.

She looks at me. "Me too."

I nod, ignoring the pang in my heart. When she exits the vehicle, the next thing I know her brothers are at my door with bright, eager smiles. In their hands they hold a case of beer and pizza. To celebrate.

Fuck me. They didn't know. Nette must not have told them — and I was too consumed by drowning my fears in the comfort of her body. Besides, I'm not used to "family" who celebrates with you. Mine is always competing and trying to tear each other apart.

"Come on, man. I heard you are gonna officially be family now, so let's party!"

Nette sucks in a deep breath and looks at me. Both of us, a deer — a panther — caught in headlights. "Uh.... I really want to..."

"And you're going to," Nette says with a bright smile. "Like you said, everything is still right on track."

"So, I'm coming inside..." I trail off, eyeing her response tentatively.

"You might wanna park your Tesla in the garage though... no way it's gonna be safe out here."

"Yeah. Let's do that. Don't want anyone to steal my baby."

Nette laughs. "Sweetie, no one wants your car. They just hate you. They'll probably spray paint obscenities on it."

Of course, they hate me. I can't help but wonder if her family that is so kindly welcoming me inside their home despite everything would hate me too if they knew what happened tonight.

Nette's mother wraps me in a warm hug as soon as I step inside. It's too much. "I should probably let you know..."

Nette interrupts me. "I didn't feel comfortable letting him make his announcement tonight. We still are fully committed to each other and plan on being mates. But, well, meeting my birth family was rough…"

That's one way to put it.

Her mother nods, and I wonder how hard this must be on her too. The complex unspoken emotions of a mother watching her daughter have another mother. I never realized it, but the night I met Nette, I was affecting more lives than just hers and mine. The guilt begins to weigh on me, and I start to wonder if perhaps Nette is the reasonable one here. Maybe I was foolish to be walking around with such hope.

I leave as early as I can without being rude — and it was strange to spend time in a family setting that didn't leave me feeling drained. I didn't want to leave! But I knew I had to get back to my father as soon as possible. Besides, I was terrible at keeping a secret. I'm not sure how her brothers didn't pick up on it — couldn't they see Nette's body language was forced? When I get to my parent's home, they open the door before I even get out of the car.

"Noah!" My mother cries, opening her arms. That's how you know it's serious. My mother is actually acting like a mother. I surprise myself by letting her embrace me.

I can remember the last time she hugged me. Ironically enough it was while Bo was living with us. He said it was a mistake, but looking back... I wonder if it really was. I had a pet dog and when it turned up dead with deep panther claw marks, my parents knew it was one of us. I knew it wasn't me.

When I broke down sobbing over Shadow's body, my mom knew too. She held me and yelled at Bo to go to our room and never come out. I was sure his parents would pick him up that night. They never did.

Strange to think he is Nette's twin. *How is she processing this?* A sharp pang of guilt reminds me to check in on her. All I did was fuck her and pretend everything is okay —

no wonder she's upset with me. I didn't even ask how she was doing, if she would be okay... I'm such a dick!

"I hate to interrupt this tender moment, but we need to make a plan."

I step back, nod at both of them, and go inside.

"I want to first say thank you, son." My father leads us to the family room and takes a seat on the oversized leopard print sofa. "I thought you hated me. I never thought you'd sacrifice your life for mine."

"And the pack," I add, hoping he knows I didn't do this for him. At least, not fully. Sure, I know some part of me — the little boy who longed for his father's approval — had a part in this decision, but I chose this for everyone.

He nods. "We must start training soon. You have a week to prepare for battle. At the very least, all you have to do is survive for ten minutes."

And not kill Nette's father for 10 minutes. It's the unspoken part that destroys me, because what if I fail? What if I kill her father? What if the panther takes over? I suck in a sharp breath as all the dreams of marrying Nette and having a family fade and all I can see is the heartbreak and betrayal on her face as I kill the man who is the reason for her existence.

"It's going to be okay," my mom says, and I ache at how artificial she sounds when providing comfort. I think Nette's mother and brothers love authentically, fearlessly. I wonder what it's like to be loved your whole life without restraint.

CHAPTER TWO

NETTE

"Why do I feel like we're missing the full story, Nette?" Mom places a steaming cup of hot cocoa in front of me. I watch the marshmallows melt and swirl with the cinnamon. I sigh.

"Because you only have the G rated trailer for whatever this shit show is," I confess. My eyes burn, begging me to cry, but I know if I do, I will never stop. "So much for connecting with my family. My birth parents. They're total dicks."

"Nette!" Mom slaps my wrist, causing me to nearly spill my hot cocoa. "Don't you dare talk about your family that way."

Sitting my cup down, I reach my hands around Mom's face. "You... Are... My... Family..."

Tears brim in her eyes. "Nette. You can have more than one family."

She is right. Noah is my family. The people in my pack and the people I help at the non-profit are my family. But the people I met last night? My parents? No.

"They are not my family." With a deep breath and a deep sense of detachment, I relay the events of not only tonight but the last few weeks to my mother. I do not spare a single detail — except for maybe the spicy ones.

"Oh, honey. They sound absolutely terrible! What horrible people. She just... it was all some sick little game." Mom shakes her head. "Well, I am glad of all the places, she chose me."

I nod. "Me too."

"What about Noah, honey? How is he doing? Oh dear, and we dragged him in here to celebrate! No wonder he was in such a hurry to leave."

I laugh. "I think it was good for him to be around some normal people for once. His parents are just as bad as my birth parents."

"Oh, I wouldn't say we're normal!"

"I mean, it's more normal than killing people off. Think about it, we don't even have a pack leader... I guess you're kind of our leader..."

"Oh, well, in that case. I'm pissed off with Mabel for stealing my family recipe and using it at her diner. I think we should employ that... What did you call it? Law 82? 72? Law pooh pooh!"

We break into a fit of giggles and I am so glad I didn't grow up with my birth family. So glad that I know kind-ness and light and hope and love.

"How have things been going at Helping Hands?" I ask. It's been a minute since I've checked in on our non-profit. A knife named Guilt stabs me in the chest — I've aban-doned everything I fought for. In a good way, but also, it feels so misguided.

"It's been going wonderful. About that, you are still our main gal. Along with me, of course. You know, your brother has been eyeing your office every day since you left."

"I told him he could use it…"

"I know but he says he doesn't want something he doesn't have the title for."

"What a drama queen!"

"Did you just call me a drama queen?" my brother says.

"How long have you been standing there?" I gasp.

"Long enough to hear you call me a drama queen."

"Well, Sir Drama Queen, I'd like to officially bestow upon you, my title. You can take my office at Helping Hands, okay?" I hope he didn't hear everything else… I don't want him to worry about this crazy pack mess with MidnightZ.

"Are you sure? I mean, are you not coming back?"

"I'll volunteer as often as I can, but Mom is right. You guys got this under control. And working at MidnightZ and my new life…it takes up so much of my time."

"My new life! Ha! You hear that?" My brother scoffs, pointing at me and looking over at mom. *Good*, I breathe. He didn't hear — and if I have any say in the matter, no one other than Mom will know the fate that awaits me if Noah fails. At least not until it's come to pass.

"Oh, shut up!" I force a smile and throw a light punch into his arm.

"Our sweet Nette is all grown up now and fancy!"

"I will be checking in regularly..." I warn with a teasing wink. If everything falls apart, I may be checking in sooner than later, embracing my old life once again...

I'm not sure what I expected when I stepped into the office, but being pulled aside from HR for a meeting was definitely not it. "After speaking with Noah and other concerned parties, we have decided that you should work in another department. Third floor. It's our outreach de-partment. You'll be helping our social media team. Don't worry! We'll train you. And Noah said you have excellent experience working for a non-profit that you created!"

"He did, did he?" I ask, blushing. Fidgeting, I wish I could stand tall in my accomplishments, because being humble didn't bode well in a job setting. I've always been confident and proud of my achievements, but I always found it hard to display that pride.

"He sure did! Here, let me show you to your new office."

"Office?" I bite my lip to keep my jaw from dropping. Is an office going to the new girl going to help work politics? Doubtful.

"Don't worry. It's nothing special. Everyone in that department has their own office. Someone did a study about how having your own space is great for productivity, so while Noah's dad was still CEO, he decided to implement that strategy on the third floor."

"Oh, wow," I say with fake enthusiasm to cover the relief I feel. *Good. I won't stand out.*

"I know. It's lame. As if he cares about anything other than the results of his productivity."

"I, uh..."

"I also heard you and Noah got in a wicked fight. Something to do with your birth parents. And his father! But that's beside the point, and I am not bringing it up to gossip. I mean, I would never." *Sure....* "But it's caused quite a distraction for this floor. So yeah, let's get you to your new office. You'll love it!" She all but squeals as she rambles on about how much I'll love this and how lucky I am.

As she leads me to the elevators, all eyes are on me once again. I can't tell if they pity me or envy me. Or maybe they just hate me. Jutting my chin up, I decide right then, I don't care. I am making enough money to keep my family out of poverty, continue to fund the non-profit, and be in a position where I can make changes from within.

Having a private office is a blessed relief from all the whispering gossip and prying eyes. I do my best to pay attention to my training, and I can tell by my superior's tone she doubts my capability.

"I am Tracy. I know you managed a non-profit before this but working at MidnightZ whether in this position or even as a secretary, it's a lot of work. Most girls don't last. Even before the layoffs, we had a high turnover. Don't let those handout-seeking panthers who made it to your non-profit fool you. Those who belong here stay here. Even when things get tough, and we have to keep a tight ship."

I open my mouth to correct her, but before I can even get a syllable out Tracy continues. "You have ten modules, each about an hour in length. I want them completed by the end of your shift today."

I gape. How am I ever going to have time to learn about the panther pack and try to save Noah? Will I even have time to spend with him before... well, before I might not ever be able to again.

"Done!" I announce, half expecting a round of cheers to celebrate my success as I submit the last module. It takes me longer than anticipated - twelve hours, not ten. I reach for my cell phone and begin typing out a text to Noah, surprised he hadn't said anything all day. Before I finish typing out my message, I hear a sharp knock on my office door.

"I am finished, Tracy," I say, annoyed. When I look up I realize it's not Tracy at all. "Oh, Mrs. Kahan. I am so sorry. I didn't realize..."

"I see you've already got quite the promotion." She winks, a wicked smile accompanying the compliment.

"It's amazing what a little work drama can do for your career." I laugh, trying to break the tension. After all, it's my birth father that is putting her son's life at risk.

"You mean sleeping with the CEO." She laughs, and when I blush, she pats my shoulder. "As if we haven't already gone over this. Besides, there's nothing about sex to be ashamed about. I've had quite the health sex life as a young panther. Even now as a —"

"I'm sure you do," I cut her off.

"Listen, Nette. I am worried about my son. As you know, he signed his life away the other night."

"For his father," I add, knowing full well if I never stumbled into his life, this wouldn't be happening.

"For my husband," she agrees. "Don't let him fool you. This isn't some little playground fight."

"I figured. Speaking of some of your ways... Well, forgive me, but I've heard all of my life that shifters like my brothers — wolves — and other species are considered to be monsters by the panther community."

She nods. "And you would argue that it is we, who are the monsters."

"You're going to let your own son die over some squabble?" I ask, trying to prove my point. My mother would never do such a thing, I want to add, but I know better. Mrs. Kahan is not a woman to be messed with.

"He is not going to die, Nette," she responds firmly. The conviction in her voice is a clear defense mechanism, and I can feel the pain laced in each word. If she wasn't such a cold-hearted bitch, I'd give her a hug. I'd tell her it's okay to not be okay. I wonder if anyone has ever shown her such kindness.

"Sorry," I mumble.

"As you should be." She breathes, collecting herself — her eyes glazing over, and I wonder where it is she goes to calm down. Somehow, I don't imagine Mrs. Kahan is the type to picture a calming sunset to bring her nerves under control. I try so hard to humanize her, because I know underneath every monster there was once a child who believed in magic, hope, and love.

"I just don't understand why wolves and other shifters are considered less than, when all we've done is the bare minimum to survive. Whereas you have these strange rules, and well quite frankly, a great deal of corruption both in your pack, Mr. Kahan's policies for all shifters in the area, and MidnightZ."

When Mrs. Kahan attempts to respond, I raise my hand. "No. I mean, I know you're like the Alpha's wife and my soon-to-be mate's mother, but no. I am talking here. I know you are a dangerous woman. I know I almost died because of you. I know that your husband has risked Noah's life on multiple occasions. What I don't understand is why is this time different? Why have you been letting me into your circle... Why are you fighting for your son now?"

"Clarity is in death," she whispers.

And the pieces fall into place at an accelerating speed. "Mr. Kahan is dying."

"Yes." She breathes, her teeth graze her lips. I didn't expect to see her cry, but I certainly did not expect to see her speak so coolly on such a matter. "As I am sure Noah has told you, we are aware of the corruption that extends far beyond us. If you think we are bad, I guarantee you that your birth parents... they are so much worse. My husband would not be able to withstand this fight. He would die."

'Does Noah know?"

"No. Rebellious, but a good one he is. He knew that should his father fail; your father would be made Alpha."

"And that would be bad..."

"Very."

"It's a blessing Noah volunteered himself and that his offer sufficed."

"Does he stand a chance?"

"Like I said, he won't die. But this is a serious battle."

I knew that was a promise she couldn't keep. He could die, or she wouldn't be here. But who has the heart to admit that kind of truth to themselves?

"What can I do?" I ask, sure to match her tone of authority.

"Give him space. He will need every minute he can to train and prepare. I will allow you to visit him for one hour per day."

"You will allow me?" I scoff.

She doesn't even flinch. "After he wins, you two can do whatever you want. Fuck until the sun goes down and pop out fifty little panthers. But my son will not die because of you. If he hadn't met you, none of this would be happening. Your parents are trying to make a point."

"You invited me to work here. You made my presence known —"

"Your presence was known before that, child."

"I... Am... Not... A... Child..." I spit through gritted teeth. She raises her brow at me, and I can't tell if she admires my defiance or is contemplating doing away with me right here. I didn't care. I continue, "Can't you just abolish this stupid law?"

"There is a small faction within our pack that would ensure the battle happened one way or another. Panthers don't back out on their vows."

"You guys are a fuckin' trip, you know that right?"

She rolls her eyes, and I could picture her being one of those 90s villain mothers with a glass of wine and a cigarette in hand as she scolded her children. Throw in a pink fuzzy robe or a coat made of wolf shifters, and she'd fit the role perfectly. "And it works. I mean, darling, we have everything that everyone else wants."

"At what cost?" I ask, as she walks away.

"Whatever it takes. Noah will be here to pick you up soon. Be ready. You only have one hour with him."

"Does he know that?"

"We met this morning. He knows everything I told you and more."

I huff. "He better survive."

"He will. So long as you don't distract him, he will."

"You can't know that. You know that you can't know that."

She rolls her eyes and without so much as another word, she leaves. I get a ping on my computer, a notification from Tracy asking for an update on my work. *Fuck.* Balancing work and trying to keep your boyfriend alive is a bit too much for a Monday.

"Are you sure I can leave my car here overnight?" I ask tentatively.

Noah chuckles. "Love, no offense, but no one in this building is gonna steal your car. And I am certainly not going to find you."

"Ha. ha." I slip off my shoes. My feet ache from wearing heels all day — so not me! I miss the sneakers and ballet flats I wore on my days at the non-profit. "I *meant* that no one would tow it. I know my car isn't fancy like yours, Mr. Tesla Owner."

"I know," he teases.

"Your mom is kind of a bitch, by the way."

"Nette!" he slams the brakes, and my heart drops to my stomach. Maybe I crossed a line... "You really just said that." He laughs and laughs. "I know, I know. She is. God, I guess that woman can bring out the beast in anyone."

"It's contagious," I admit.

"Well, at least my parents aren't trying to kill you anymore."

"She said we have an hour," I say, as if this limitation compares to being murdered. It feels a lot alike.

"Ugh, that. What are they gonna do? Come break down my door and drag me off your beautiful body."

"Noah!" It was my turn to gasp at what was definitely not an image I ever needed in my mind.

"Let me handle my parents. They're over dramatic. It's just a silly fight."

"Uh huh..."

As I slip off his shirt, I am taken aback by the bruising and scars on his body. "Noah..."

"It's just from training. MMA fighters get bruised up all the time in training. It's no big deal."

My fingers dance across the scars that I'm sure were gaping wounds hours earlier — he heals faster than a human. I suppose I do too. "Did your father do this?"

"It's routine. Now can we please enjoy this cabin. I need a break. You need a break..."

"Noah, you don't have to be strong for me," I plead.

"I'm not," he growls. Sucking in sharp breath, he sighs. "It's complicated, Nette. I am sorry for snapping at you. Can we please just fuck?"

I tilt my head. "I mean, who am I to deny a totally-not-going-to-die man his last wishes?"

Noah pulls me hard against his chest, his teeth grazing at my neck and biting until small pin pricks of blood peek out. "Mm," he moans, and licks at the wounds before pushing me away. As he falls to his knees, he pulls my skirt and panties down with him. Each movement is rapid, jarring, and delightful. He kisses and bites my thighs as he makes his way up higher and higher.

His tongue draws sensuous circles around my clit, as I grip fistful of hair in my hands, feeling my claws peeking out.

"Noah, please," I beg. I've waited all day for him, clenching my thighs together when that heat-rush of need flowed over me. But now I had him and sure, there was a lot I wanted to talk to him about, but we only had an hour... *Fuck it*. The heavy conversations can wait. I need this. I need *him*. He continues to make love to me with his mouth, and I quiver uncontrollably. Just as I am on the edge of unraveling under his lips, Noah pulls away. He rips his jeans off in a swift movement only a shifter man would be capable of.

All of the worry and pain dissipates as his body enters mine, his claws escaping and digging into my skin. "Noah," I cry out. My hips meeting his, consumed by the power that is our love, our bodies fitting together so perfectly like an erotic game of Tetris.

Chapter Three

Noah

If there is a cure for imminent death, it's burying myself in this woman's body. Fuck. I moan with each wild thrust of her hips, biting my lips to keep from giving into exactly what she wants — I will drag this out. Each moment. Each moment we have left, and fuck, I hope it's more than just a few more days. Because if we fuck, consumed by our patience, we won't have to talk. I pull her body off my cock and lift her up, delighting in her whimper of unmet need. "Patience, love."

She opens her mouth, and I feel the words before she says them. No. Not now. Before she can even mention our time limit, I have her legs draped around me and her clit pressed against my tongue once again. Nette's shivers cause my body to quiver and my cock to tighten with need. I lick, tease, and suck her clit, sliding my fingers inside — one, then two. Her hips arch, and her hands grip my neck, pushing me deeper still. "Noah don't stop. Please don't stop."

I had other plans — I planned to stop, but at that moment, I didn't. I give in, licking faster, thrusting my fingers faster, until she comes hard and fast. Breathless, I pull myself away and hover over her. I enter her slowly, my fingers teasing her clit again, her legs instantly tensing. "More?" she cries, and I can't tell if she is asking how she can possibly experience more pleasure. Or if she is begging for more, but the need in her eyes and the arch in her hips is clear.

I feel her hands reach down and cup my sac in between thrusts. Teasing, delicate, until her hands fall away, trembling. She is close again — I can feel it as she tightens around me. I slow my fingers' rhythm and my thrusts. "Nette," I whisper, reaching my free hand to lift her chin up. "I... Will... Never... Stop..."

She tilts her head. I can't finish the sentence because I don't know what I mean — stop loving her? Stop fucking her? Stop pleasuring her? Fighting for her? All the above? Yes, that. All the above, I want to tell her. I will not stop loving her. Stop fucking her. Stop living. I will survive this for her. I hope she can feel the words pour from my body. A promise that feels written in the stars, but I know as soon as the high of our pleasures fade, reality will whisper to me once again.

But for now, the raw need in her eyes, the understanding only our bodies can communicate. I pick my pace up once more. "Fuck. Fuck. Fuck." I moan and growl, gnash and shiver.

"Oh," Nette cries out. "Fuck yes."

Our bodies shiver and collapse into each other.

"That was... intense," Nette whispers before bursting into giggles.

"Well, we've been apart for over 24 hours..."

"Which is torture. I might die from that alone," she comments, gently trying to bring up the topic at hand.

I dismiss her. "Let me go back to get us some dinner. I already sent my parents a text that I am missing their little curfew by a few minutes…"

"How long have we been fucking?" she asks with a giggle.

"For a hot minute." I wink. "What do you want to eat?"

"I actually already ate dinner at work," Nette says, slipping on her clothes. I follow suit and we make our way back downstairs.

I need to do something with my hands. Something with her body or my body, and since we're both spent when it comes to sex, cooking seemed logical. "You wanna go for a run?"

"A run! It's freezing outside!"

"Not if you have a fur coat." I wink.

"I've never really shifted much," she admits weakly.

"Are you… embarrassed?"

"You've seen me before," she snaps. "I'm not embarrassed."

"What is it?" I ask gently.

"It feels animalistic to shift in the middle of the woods."

"Bo and I used to shift like this. In these woods."

"My brother. God, that feels weird to say." She laughs, but it's the kind of laugh when everything is falling apart and it's the only thing you can do. "You have more of a relationship with my brother than I probably ever will."

"You're not missing out," I promise.

"It doesn't sound like it. I mean, it does sound like it. That I am missing out. When you talk about him, you sound sad. Like you miss him." Nette walks up to where the photo sits of Bo and I as kids and picks it up. "He does look like me."

"Twins are like that." I tease.

She scowls at me before returning her gaze to the photo. "Do you think he'd be the way he is if he didn't grow up with *them*?"

"That's the question that haunts all of society, isn't it? How much of us is our circumstances and how much is DNA?"

Nette flinches.

"Don't worry, hun." I pull her into a hug. "You are nothing like them. You will never be."

"I guess I've always been afraid to be in my panther form," she admits. "Most of my community hated panthers. And quite frankly, so did I. What if I am the monster? What if I lose myself and become what I hate?"

"You should love every part of yourself, Nette. You are fucking perfect."

"I'm perfect, I know," she says with a cheesy smile. "But really I've already sold out, haven't I? Working a job at MidnightZ, befriending your mother to some extent..."

"Shh." I reach for her hands and pull them close to my face. "We are not our parents. We are us. I am me. And you are you. And we are together."

And with that, we strip off our clothes once more and step outside in the cold for one shocking blistering moment before shifting into our truest forms. We run in the snow and through the woods, our hearts racing and our minds connected in a deep and powerful way, where we do not need words to communicate. It's beautiful to watch her fall into comfort with her panther form. Her steps tentative at first, cautious, before she lets go and embraces herself.

When we get back, the sun is coming up. "Well, I definitely missed curfew by more than a few minutes."

She laughs. "Your mom is gonna kill me."

"Don't worry about her. I'll tell her I fell asleep after you left and forgot — "I pause. Nette holds her hand up as if to shush me.

"Did you leave the door open?" Nette asks, picking up her pile of clothes, shaking them free of snow and slipping them on. I do the same. The icy sensation is nothing compared to the chill that runs down my spine.

"What? No. I even locked it..."

But she is right. The door is open. And someone else is here. I can feel it. Smell it. The smell is so familiar, yet I can't seem to place it. Not until I see his shadow approaching.

"Hello, brother." Bo says, standing in the doorway. "And sister."

"Bo," I answer calmly, with a slow nod of my head.

Bo had always had a strange and dangerous nature to him, far more intense than other shifters in the pack. Even as kids. As a teenager, he earned the reputation as a mama's boy, an outsider, aloof.

"She shouldn't be here," Bo continues. "Mom should've just killed her."

I growl, ready to show him which one of them should be dead.

Chapter Four

Nette

I've been the subject of a lot of nasty behaviors in my life — the cruelest words have been wrapped around my soul since childhood. My mama tried her best to shield me from the hate and showered me with extra love, but the older I got, the more I was subject to hatred. But to hear my own long-lost brother say my birth mother should've killed me. Ouch. That hit different.

Before I can address him, let alone process what he said, Noah is shifting back into a panther and lunging at Bo. Bo shifts immediately and dodges his attack. I stand there, barely clothed, shivering as snow encircles me and the traumatic fight unfolding before my eyes. Bo's claws dig deep into Noah's back, sure to leave yet another wound. This seems unfair to attack Noah before his big battle.

This must break some law! I cry out, pleading, "Stop. Stop. Stop!"

But they don't listen.

I run inside, slam the door behind me, and lock it. I rifle through my belongings until I find my cell phone and call Noah's parents.

"Where is he?" his mother seethes a greeting.

"It's Bo." I say, my voice shaking and my hands trembling so much I drop the phone. When I pick it up, I can hear Mrs. Kahan screaming obscenities.

"They're fighting. It's bad."

"Goddammit, child. We have a pack member that lives nearby. They'll be over soon. We'll be driving up now." Mrs. Kahan scolds me for spending more than an hour with him before the phone clicks.

How is this my fault? Another voice chimes in, asking *how is it not*. If Noah hadn't met me none of this would be happening. I know that in my soul. He would be living a shallow life, but a safe life. Taking over his dad's company, without some forbidden fruit ruining his life with the promise of knowledge, passion, and love.

I hear gunshots and two distinct yelps. I rush outside to see a burly old man bundled up in flannel and a wool coat. His curly hair sticking out at all angles as the snow clings to it and his beard. "Children," he bellows. "It's about time you two stop fighting." He looks at me, "You must be Nette. Nice to meet ya. Sorry you're gettin' to see the worst of our kind with Bo here. We ain't all like that"

As if the Kahan's have been welcoming, but this man is so strange. He isn't like the Kahan's or the other panthers I've met. He reminds me of a man my mother used to spend time with. He'd take us kids out hunting and fishing with him, seeing the good in everyone, living off the land, and determined to teach others how to do the same.

"Are they okay? Did you shoot them?" I ask, breathless.

"Shoot them? Oh these? They're just tranquilizers. Ain't no way I could take out a full-grown panther at my age. Let alone two!" He laughs, a deep comforting roar.

"Let's get your boy in. Bo can sleep it off outside. Maybe it'll teach him to not be so reckless."

We work together to drag Noah inside. It's strange carrying what feels like a lifeless panther body, and I can't help but fear I will carry him like this again when he fights my birth father. I do my best to quiet the thought. "Noah, sweetie," I whisper after we lay him down. "It's gonna be alright." I know he can't hear me, but I need to hear the words spoken, because it certainly doesn't feel like.

"You really did enter this scene at a complicated time, huh? Let me introduce myself. My name is Robbie. Been friends with the Kahan's since they were just kiddos themselves. Times sure have changed for us folk." His contagious, familiar laughter wraps around me like a warm hug. "How 'bout we brew us some coffee until his folks get here?"

I make my way to the kitchen. I keep glancing at the door.

"Don't worry, they won't be wakin' up for a while. Bo's out for at least another hour."

"No offense, but you don't seem like the Kahan's." I say, doing my best to focus on the task of making coffee.

He bellows a deep roar of a laugh again. It's comforting. He reminds me of the fatherly types that stayed with us growing up. "Well, I never did get into those nasty politics. You know the Kahan's weren't always so..."

"Corrupt," I finish coldly.

"Now, now. We all can become the monster of our stories if pushed hard enough."

I frown. That was my biggest fear. "Did you hear about Noah's fight?"

"Unfortunately. I sure hope he survives."

I blanch. "He will." At this moment I understand his mother in a strange new way. She said the same thing -and I knew why, but I hated her for not accepting my fear as valid. Yet here I was doing the same. As much as we doubt and want to be realistic, to hear someone else speak of our fears... Well, that is unacceptable.

I pour each of us a cup of coffee. We take tentative sips, warming up from the cold. "I saw you two shifting in the woods. Would you believe it that I used to run around those woods? That's when I met her..."

"Her?" I ask.

He shakes his head. "Ah, I've said too much. His parents should be here soon. You should get cleaned up. I'll keep an eye on the boy. They won't be waking up anytime soon."

"Are you sure?" I ask. He's assured me multiple times now, but I just can't shake the fear of Bo waking up before Noah's parents get here.

"Sure am! Go shower, get warmed up, and maybe not mention having been out there shifting in the woods with Noah when his parents get here. We panthers may be into some weird shit, but it's that kind of behavior that raises some red flags if you know what I mean."

I don't, but I can't. Time is short, and he is right, I need to clean up before his parents get here.

I don't realize how cold I am, how much my body is shivering until the steaming hot water hits it, washing away the fear and ice from my skin.

When I come back downstairs, his mother is in the kitchen. Sipping coffee with the man that saved our lives. Her body language is different than I've ever seen - at ease, gentle. She stiffens the moment she notices me. "There you are," she huffs.

"We didn't mean to—"

"We'll discuss this later."

Robbie winks at me, as if to say it'll be fine, and not to pay her any thought, but she didn't try to kill him like she did me! "Where is Noah?" I ask.

"His father is taking him home."

"And Bo?"

"I'll deal with Bo in the mornin'." Robbie waves dismissively.

I try to accept this - accept that everything is okay, but my body was still reeling from the events. Once I get inside Mrs. Kahan's car, she rolls her eyes. "Are you taking any of this seriously, Nette? For god's sake, Noah could've died. Bo has no sense of..."

"Morality?" I add.

"And he's your brother... Do you know how much that frightens me?"

"I'm not like him," I snap.

"Then stop putting my son's life at risk."

Mrs. Kahan drops me off at home. "I'll have a car pick you up for work tomorrow. I will be increasing security at the office. Both you and Noah are not to be alone at any point."

Strange how we've gone from his family being a threat to protecting me. "Understood. Mrs. Kahan, I am so sorry."

"Don't."

I bow my head down, appearing submissive, but the guilt weighs down on me.

"Don't," she continues more gently, "let it happen again."

I nod. "I promise I won't. Thank you."

"I'll station a guard outside your family home as well. Call us if you need anything. You did the right thing to call me."

"Thank you."

"Also, Nette... here." She hands me a black envelope. "Open this. Not here. Go inside first. Please consider it."

When I get inside, I dial a number from Bo's phone. While he was unconscious, I grabbed it. Although no one saw me pick it up, and at first, I thought it was my own until it didn't request my face ID or even a password. I select the contact that says Mom and let it ring.

"Bo! Finally, where were you? We were so worried. Someone called and said you were heading up to Kahan's cabin. Why? Why would you do that?"

"This isn't Bo," I answer ominously.

A tense silence fills the space between me and the speaker. "Nette."

"Your son is fine. I mean, he was tranquilized after trying to attack me and Noah. He's out in the snow by the cabin for, I don't know, three hours now. He'll be waking up soon."

"What do you want?"

"I want you to leave Noah alone. Call off this stupid fight."

She laughs. "Oh sweetie. That's adorable. Fearless. I like it."

"I'm not joking."

"I know. That's what makes this even more delightful."

"You owe me this much," I snap. My resolve breaks and tears fill my eyes.

"Oh, love. I owe you nothing. You're lucky to even be alive."

Click... I throw the phone across the phone.

"Holy mother of Mary, Nette! Trying to kill me with this thing, are you?" My mother gasps, holding up the phone. "This thing is broken. Honey, are you okay?"

"It's not my phone," I answer. "Don't worry about it."

"Okay, Nette. We did the whole rage thing in high school. You're a big girl now. What's going on?"

"Just got off the phone with my birth mom." I catch my mother up to speed and when I see her wide eyes, I realize I should tone it back a bit. Surely this woman's heart can't take much more. "I'm really just overreacting, but it's a lot."

She nods. "And what is this?" She picks up the black envelop Mrs. Kahan gave it to me. "It looks like an invitation."

I forgot all about it. "I'm not sure," I answer.

Mom gives me a kiss goodnight and when she leaves the room, I break the golden seal on the envelope. Inside a thick embossed card.

Nette,

You are formally invited to join the Midnight Shadows Pack. You may retain your membership with Lone City Wanders Pack should that be compliant with their individual policies and regulations. Upon your acceptance, you will also act as a liaison between the packs, facilitating peace and progress among the shifters of this city.

Yours Truly,

Mr. and Mrs. Kahan

"Well, you weren't wrong," I whisper but no one can hear me. "It is an invitation, but I'm not sure if it's one I am ready to accept right now..." I wish I could tell someone about this — and though I know my mother would be supportive, I'm not about to pull her back in here. It's late. She needs sleep. I need sleep. And my brothers? They're so out of the loop it would take me all day to catch them up to speed. What would I say? Oh, by the way, your soon-to-be brother-in-law is actually risking his life and might die in a few days? I laugh out loud, pondering what my life has become.

When did life get so complicated?

I spent the rest of the morning catching up on sleep, tossing and turning, reliving carrying Noah's frame, consumed by how lifeless it felt.

Chapter Five

Noah

Darkness shifts to light and my heavy eyes finally open completely. "Mother?" I ask, blinking. My last memory is fucking Nette. This makes no sense. Did my mother come through on her little Cinderella time-limit policy? *Ugh.* I hope she wasn't too mean to Nette. It wasn't her fault... I struggle to remember what happened next. When did Nette and I call it a night...

I lift my arm and wince. "Jesus. These fights with dad are leaving me broken. I can't even lift my arms!" I examine the giant bruise on my shoulder. Is that dried blood on my hands?

"That one is from Bo," my mother comments. "Do you not remember?"

I shake my head, and everything continues to shake after I stop. My body, the bed I am sitting on, and the surrounding walls. Was I drunk? "Bo?" I ask.

"Robbie's tranquilizers," she laughs. "I always forget how strong they are. It'll come back to you in a day or two. Bo crashed your little party with Nette. Sweetie, I want you here as much as possible, not just to train and prepare, but to keep you both safe."

Though the memories are scattered, the pieces fall into place. "Bo attacked us?" I ask. "Oh, my god. Is Nette okay?"

"Thankfully, yes."

"Where is she?"

"She is home. Her home. I stationed a guard outside and we will have one of our trusted drivers pick her up in the morning." Mom breathes, holds up her hand to wave. My father steps in. "We also gave her an invitation. *The invitation.*"

"To the pack?" I ask, astonished. For some reason, I thought the only way she would join would be to mate with me and sacrifice her position with the Lone City Wanderers. I say as much, and my mother explains they made an exception.

"I'm surprised." I look over at my father. "And you're okay with this? What is the trick?"

"People change, son," he says weakly. "There is no trick."

I tilt my head. But this much change? Something feels off, and being a Kahan, I couldn't help but voice it. "Since when? You were set in your archaic ways from the day I was born."

"That's enough!" my mother snaps. "You will not speak to your father like this."

Before I can tell her I have every right to speak to him the way I want, he coughs. "It's been a long night and I seem to have come down with a cold. If I didn't have to walk around in the snow to deal with you and Bo..." He huffs. Since when do shifters come down with colds? He's clearly just trying to get out of the conversation.

"Just let it be," my mother chimes in again. "There is no catch. And you should call and let Nette know you're okay. Tell her thank you, because if she hadn't called us in time to get Robbie out to you... you would be dead. If not, both of you."

I rifle for my cellphone once my parents leave the room. I'm still dizzy, but I manage to hit dial on her contact.

"Noah!" she cries. "I am so glad you're safe."

"Me too. I don't remember much... I know what happened. Mom told me." I catch my breath. "She said I'll remember in a day or two when the tranquilizer wears off. So much for training." I laugh. "Maybe we can spend more time together while I recover."

"No." Nette says firmly. "Your mom is right. It's safer this way."

"Safer?"

"You almost died, Noah. If Robbie hadn't stepped in..."

"If I can't defeat Bo," I scowl, my ego wounded, "how the fuck am I going to defeat his father? He's far more experienced..."

"You will. I didn't mean it like that, Noah. Just... let yourself heal and train, because if last night taught me anything, it's that I can't bear to lose you."

"You won't lose me," I respond softly.

"I know. That's why you need to focus."

My mother was right. It took me a few days to remember what happened out at the cabin. All the while, I did my best to avoid Nette. It took a great number of cold showers and converting my sexual frustrations into working out and training. I am exhausted, but not weakened.

"You should spend these last days recovering with minimal training," my father notes.

"Can I spend this time with Nette?" I ask. I feel like a foolish little boy asking to spend time with his girlfriend, but I needed to know it was safe to do so. For both her and for me.

"You may," my father concedes, and for a moment I wonder if this is like agreeing to let an inmate on death row have his last meal.

"Dad," I ask, "Are you sure you are, okay?"

"Are you disrespecting me, son?" He raises his voice. "I am just fine. Go. Get out of here."

"Oh... Okay. Whatever then." I step outside the room when I hear him coughing again. Strange. Perhaps his rage is leading him to these fits. Whatever the reason, I am eager to see Nette. My body ached for her, and I had been waiting far too long to embrace her once again and forget for just a brief moment in time what awaits me.

I grab my keys, ready to head out, when my mother stops me. "Your father and I just want you to be happy. You know that, right? Every choice we made was for you. For your safety."

I tilt my head. "You sure had a weird way of going about it."

"We did what we had to do with the lives we were given. So did you. So did Nette..."

"Why are you guys acting so weird?"

My mom's eyes fill with tears. "I'm scared," she whispers. It's a rare moment of vulnerability.

I sigh. Of course, she is scared of what I am. That I will die. "I'll be okay, Mom." I promise, "I won't fail this battle. And I won't get hurt going out with Nette tonight, but even Dad agrees I need a break."

She nods. "Of course." She wipes her tears away and puts her fierce facade back in place. "Your curfew still applies. We've been keeping close tabs on Bo, but you never know what this family will pull."

"I'll be home before you know it."

"Has Nette talked to you at all about the invitation?" she asks.

"Has she not accepted yet?" I ask.

"I haven't heard anything from her since that night."

"I'm sure she's just processing it all." But for some reason, I start to worry. What if she's changed her mind?

And who would blame her if she did?

Chapter Six

Nette

I ignore the incessant honking outside. I don't even have the luxury to be late to work or lie that I am sick with all eyes on me. I slam my spoon into my cheerios. "Ugh!" I groan.

"Work sucks," my brother chimes in.

"I would give anything to be back at the non-profit right now."

He laughs. "Hey, you accepted the job offer. And from what I hear you have another invitation to accept."

"I haven't yet," I answer. "Who told you about the other invitation?"

Honk.

I look over at my mom, who is hunched over the kitchen sink doing dishes. Of course, she couldn't keep this one a secret. I let it slide, and ask, "Mom, if you knew something about someone's parents that they should know, would you tell them?"

"Like what?" Mom asks.

"Like a health thing."

"Oh! Do spill the tea!" My brother interrupts.

If I did that, I'd have to spill so much more that I've kept him out of the loop on.

Honk.

"If it's not your secret to tell, hun, you shouldn't. And you should probably go outside before they send an army to break down the door to make sure you're okay."

"When did life become so complicated?" I throw my hands up, grab the designer bag that Noah bought me, and reach for my keys.

"Really, Nette?" My brother laughs.

"You have no idea what it's like!" I wave my keys at him before storming out.

Honk.

"I am literally coming!" I shout. I am growing incredibly tired of MidnightZ guards checking in on us.

"Not yet, but you will be." Noah calls out, his head leaning outside the car window.

"Noah!" I gasp. It's been days with minimal contact. Days with drowning myself in work and pretending that my life did not take such a crazy turn. "It's so good to see you!" I run up to him and kiss his lips hard. "God, I missed you." It takes everything in my body to pull myself away from him. If I could, I'd melt into him forever — it destroyed me to not be with him, to have my last memory being his unconscious body.

"Missed me or my body?" he teases.

"Both," I answer confidently. "It's nice seeing you upright."

"It's nice being upright." He caresses my cheek. "Have you been doing, okay? I know what happened was traumatic for both of us."

"Mm," I lean into his caress. "I'm just glad you're okay. I'm surprised you're here. Your evil parents let you out of the tower?" I tease.

"With my fight right around the corner, I thought we could spend some time together."

"You didn't sneak out, did you? I don't need to piss your mom off again."

"No. I surprisingly had her blessing. Even more surprisingly, my fathers..." He shakes his head, as if processing his father's strange behavior — but I know.

I know why he is showing kindness in a new, strange way. I remind myself of my mother's words, *it's not my secret to tell.* Surely, they will tell him eventually, right?

"Let's spend time together, okay! Just nothing up at the cabin." I answer, before walking around and getting in the passenger side. "Wait. What about work? Does this mean I have the day off?"

"Yes, it does! See, dating the CEO does have perks other than almost being murdered sometimes." Noah winks before hitting the gas.

As he drives the familiar route to his place, I wait in anticipation but for what I am not sure. His body or maybe the question I know hangs on his lips. The same question that plagues my own mind. *Are you going to accept the pack invitation?*

A question I do not have the answer to. Or maybe I do, but I just don't like the answer. My whole life has changed so much since I met Noah, and I wouldn't have it any other way, but... What turned out to be just a fling between two opposites has bloomed into a dangerous delight; a love I would die for. We drive in silence until we reach his "mansion" but before we go about our sexual routine, Noah stops me.

"You don't have to tell me now. We can wait until after all is said and done. I mean, Jesus, why would you wanna be stuck in this corrupt pack if I don't survive." It's the first time I've heard him be honest about the reality of the situation that faces him, and it stings. God, it stings.

"You will survive, Noah," I correct him, the way his mother corrected me the way I corrected Robbie.

"I know, but if I don't, I need you to do something for me."

This raw, honest side of Noah frightens me. "What?" I ask.

"Don't accept the invitation. Leave. Run with your family as fast as you can. I have people who will help you. I have a place you can go. You don't have to save everyone, Nette. You've saved so many people with Helping Hands and maybe MidnightZ is too corrupt to save."

"And if you don't die?" I ask appalled. "You want me to stay in a bad situation. No, Noah. Listen. I am making the same choice regardless of whether you live or die."

He flinches.

"I didn't mean it in a bad way." I lick my lips and grab his face. "Noah, MidnightZ is corrupt. But you underestimate my ability to bring change. I don't have to save everyone. You're right. But I want to save as many people as I can. Help as many people as I can. Bring as much change as I can. That is who I am, Noah."

"I know —"

"That is why we clashed in the beginning. I am an advocate that fights against what you and your family have created." I laugh. "I'm in too deep to walk away. My roots are planted, Noah. And I will grow and bring so much light and love here."

"Fuck, I love you." He swoops me up into his arms, but we don't even make it to his bedroom. "Whatever will we do without your little sexy toy chamber," I tease.

"Oh, you underestimate me," he quips, nibbling on my ear.

I look around at the random guest room I've never seen, and begin to wonder how much of this place I've left unexamined — and wonder if one day its walls will be as familiar as my own home. I take in my surroundings, determined to be fully present in these moments — moments that deep in my soul, I know might be my last with Noah. It goes unspoken, but it's there. The room is filled with books and a woody aroma. My ass sits against the soft plush chair as his lips hang under me, grazing my thighs with his tongue, creating a delightful path to my clit.

"Oh, dammit," I moan. "I've needed you for so long." *I hope I never have to need you again.* I want to cry because I don't think I can live without Noah. Our love has been pure magic, and to go on without that, to try to find someone else... It would be impossible.

He purrs. "Me too, Nette. Me too." His whispers, and I know he knows the unspoken words my body is crying out. Each lick and caress set my body on fire, and I burn for him. I burn for him in every way possible.

He goes back to work with his tongue and fingers. Creating tentative small circles, firm, faster, before I stop him. "I want you to come inside me," I plead.

"Oh, do you now?" Noah teases. "I will," he whispers, "Just not yet."

Noah continues his assault on my clit, as I clutch the armrests of the chair, the velvety cushion as luxurious as Noah's skin. My hips arch, matching the rhythm of his mouth, of the chorus of our love until I am a crumpled, shivering mess beneath him. Before I can speak, I feel Noah's arms wrap tight around me.

He scoops me up again, carries me to his room and plops me on the bed. Hitting the switch, his "chamber" opens, and he immediately pulls out the rope. "You sounded disappointed we didn't have anything fun to play with." He teases.

"I mean..." I trail off, still shivering from his touch.

"I'll come inside, but only after you come for me three times."

"Noah. What are you some type of twisted genie?"

He nibbles on my ear, and I moan, longing for more.

"No, but I'm gonna have fun. Don't worry, you'll come a fourth time too. We have all night."

All night...those words echo in my mind.

At that moment I realize it is our last night. He ties me and I am bound to the bed as he gets to work with his mouth. I want to beg him to just fuck me, I've craved his cock for too long, but as my body quakes at his strategic movements, I succumb to it all. "Noah! Ooh!"

"Good girl," he purrs. He slides his cock in and starts round three. Determined to make him come with me before round four, I call upon my shifter strength and rip myself free from the ropes that bind me. I flip Noah underneath me and guide his cock back inside me, grabbing his hand to cup my breasts.

"Nette," he moans. "Fuck, Nette."

I smile, knowing I won this round when I feel his hips lifting to meet mine. His nails dig into my hips, guiding my faster, and my body shivers as wave upon wave of pleasure floods over me. "Noah, I'm coming."

"Fuck," he cries out, riding the wave that is my orgasm, leading him to his own. He collapses into my body, quivering in sync with me.

"I hope this never ends," I murmur.

"Shh," he pulls me into him. "Don't you feel infinite when we're with each other?"

I nod. "I feel like I can take on the world."

"Then we will. We are infinite and we will take on the world. It just so happens the world looks a lot like your birth father..."

"How do you feel with the training?" I ask, imploring. "Do you feel confident?"

"I know the future isn't here yet, but I do, Nette. I feel stronger that I ever have..."

"Kick his ass," I whisper, before falling asleep.

Suddenly my dreams shift from Noah dying to my father... My estranged birth father. I've been blaming Noah's parents for so much. I should be blaming my own.

It's 5:30 AM. In fifteen minutes, an alarm I set last night will go off to wake us both. In thirty minutes after that we will be heading to a pack location for this fight. In less than three hours, I will know if Noah is dead or alive. It's a heavy moment, but I decide to spend it watching the rise and fall of his chest. I imagine what Noah was like as a little boy. I think about the few stories he has shared with me, and the weight of Robbie's words echo in my mind. The Kahan's weren't always like this.

I wonder if his mother is awake right now, if she too is breaking at the knowledge this might be her son's last day on this earth. I grab my cellphone and slip out of bed. I call her.

"Is everything okay? Is Noah —"

I cut her off. "He is fine. I just... I figured you might be awake too."

She sighs. "He will be okay," she says, and it's a strange echo of a motherly tone I never expected to hear from her.

"He will," I repeat.

"I'll see you soon," she says firmly, her cold facade back in place.

She hangs up before I can even say goodbye.

I slip back in bed beside Noah and pretend to wake up right along with him when the alarm goes off. I pretend that I am confident and that this is just a silly little fight and soon it will all be over. I talk about how I'll accept his mother's invitation today and how he really should add more color to his kitchen. "I saw some beautiful indoor houseplants at Lowes last week..."

I've become the world's greatest pretender. My mind drifts back to Robbie once again — perhaps the Kahan's are just that. Pretenders. Good people pretending to be monsters and they pretended so long until they became one.

When we arrive at the arena, I take my seat next to Mrs. Kahan. I offer her a weak smile and she simply nods curtly. Of course, the moment we shared on the phone is long gone, but I can see the tears behind her eyes.

"He will be okay," I whisper her words back to her.

"He will." She turns and gives me the smallest of smiles, as if she is afraid what would happen if someone saw her showing kindness. Weakness.

Chapter Seven

Noah

When I was a little boy, my mother taught me to never show my tears. My father? He taught me to never show my fear. My soul is trembling, but my hands are still, firm fists at my side.

"Because Mr. Kahan has his son fighting in his place, I declare my son Bo to fight in my place."

No.

Fuck. Fuck. Fuck. I had just barely recovered from an impromptu battle with Bo...

I trained to fight someone older, someone with weak spots my father knew about. But Bo? Bo was my childhood best friend, someone who knew *my* weaknesses. Someone who nearly killed me nights before. I try to object, opening my mouth and raising my hand, but my father shushes me instantly. It's a blur of what must only be a few minutes of voting among the pack to decide if this last-minute change is acceptable. It feels like hours and seconds all at the same time. I search for Nette in the audience, and I see her gripping my mother's hand tight. They're scared, too.

When they agree that it is acceptable, Bo and I are thrown into an arena of sorts, surrounded by an audience that will either celebrate our success... or worst case, our death.

"You may fight to the death, but you only have ten minutes."

I begin my attack in human form, landing a punch right across his face. My anger and survival instinct takes over, fear melts away. I can feel my panther blood rise, demanding I protect myself. My pack. My *mate*. His words when he met Nette and I at the cabin fueled me to shift before he even gets a chance to defend himself, my panther claws lunging at his human frame. Flesh flies across the room. He cries out in pain before shifting.

Bo's weakness? He acts on impulse. He doesn't think strategically, and he thinks he can bully others into submission. He thinks I am still scared of him, but I'm not, because I have Nette, and she is worth fighting for. I fear what will happen to her if I die. The blood and pain interrupts his ability to shift as fast, and mid shift I swipe another chunk of flesh from his body, aiming for any vital organ I can.

He looks at me with sad, pleading eyes. *I'm your friend,* I can hear his mind plead with mine.

My weakness?

I care. I always care. And that second's hesitation lands me on the floor, pinned down with his sharp panther teeth inches away from my carotid. Fur covers my body, sprouting angrily, demanding me to protect myself somehow. The betrayal in that moment hurts... tears fill my large panther eyes. *It doesn't have to be that way.* My thoughts find their way into his mind, and I swear I can feel him laugh.

"Noah!" I hear Nette's voice cry out, but it feels a million miles away. It's enough, though. Enough to pull me out of my doubt, my thoughts, my feelings and fear and betrayal. I wiggle my panther form free and dig my teeth deep into him before he kicks me off. I fall hard into the rocky ground. Standing up on my four legs, I shake the dust off my fur.

We circle each other slowly. It's like a delicate dance, and all I can think of is I need to just survive for 10 minutes. I don't have to kill him. I just have to survive. I wish I knew how much more time I had, but I don't dare look at the clock and lose sight of him. I am clearly faring better than him, and this gives me hope. His body limps, oozing blood, and I hear him plead with me again.

Please. I don't want to do this either.

As if I'd fall for that again, but I can hear the edge of truth to his thoughts. He doesn't. Not really. For a second, I consider the question Nette asked: Would he be this way if he didn't grow up with the parents he did? I whimper an apology. He doesn't want to, but he will. We both know that. And my heart aches for him.

His father thought he was pulling a power move throwing Bo into the arena. A man who knows my weaknesses. A man who was so much like a brother to me. He didn't realize he was sentencing the man to his own death, because if Bo and I are alike in any way, it's that our families shaped us and broke us. I knew Bo in ways no one else ever could. Or ever would.

Only, I couldn't kill him. Even if he wasn't Nette's brother, I could never kill Bo. I just have to keep us both alive until the time runs out. *Because he was my brother.* In so many ways, despite his chaotic actions, he was always my brother.

In mere seconds, he lunges at me, I dodge. I plead with him to just give up, but he doesn't. This infuriates Bo even more. I hear chanting, or maybe it's not chanting. Words are different when you're shifted. Time is different too. It doesn't seem to quite exist. It goes by slowly, at least that's how it feels, but before you know it an entire day can pass by.

Bo jumps at me once again; this time I don't dodge before he attacks me. His claws deliver a lethal blow to my stomach. I growl, and my animalistic nature takes over.

Atta boy. Just like I used to teach you. Embrace it.

I cringe, warm liquid oozing at my sides and I deliver attack upon attack. Bo isn't moving but I can't seem to stop myself. I lunge at him and give it all I got, tearing his body apart, the copper smell of blood wrapping around me like a moldy blanket that once brought comfort before time destroyed it.

"Time! Time! Time. Fuck, Noah. We said time! Stop it. You can stop now!"

Time!

Time.

I stumble away and shift into my human form, shivering furiously. My mother rushes to me with a warm blanket. Nette at her side. I look over at Bo, and a guttural cry escapes. I turn my head to my mother instantly, sobbing hysterically. I didn't for a second care what the pack thought.

When I was a little boy, I was taught not to cry or show my fear. But now I am a man, and in front of me sits a dead man. One that I killed with my bare hands. One that I once loved like a brother. "What did I do? What did I do? I didn't want him to die."

In hindsight I could see he was delaying. He was trying to keep us both alive until the ten-minute mark.

What have I done?

They whisk Bo away, but he can't be alive... and if I killed him after the time, by default, I lost, and it will be just as bad as if I had died myself.

Nette tries to console me, whispering that it wasn't my fault, and though I squeeze her hand, I can't bear to look at her. He wasn't just my brother. He was hers.

"After reviewing the footage and discussing this matter, it has been concluded that Bo did indeed die or sustain enough injuries to cause death before the time was up. Noah did not break the rules." My father says over a loudspeaker. "This is a great loss. As you can see this battle has taken a great toll on my son. This law is archaic. It is disgusting. While I am grateful my son stepped in for me, it is time I step down."

Everyone gasps.

"Noah, son. You are next in line to be Alpha. And you have proven yourself more than worthy of that role. More human than some of the monsters in this room."

I blink, my mind still reeling from everything. With tear filled eyes, I walk to where my father stands and speak into the mic. "As many of you saw, and can still see, I am not happy with the blood that was shed today." I look into the crowd to find Bo's parents. Nette's parents. Their eyes are empty — void of tears or any emotion. "I am mourning someone who was one of my best friends. Bo got the short end of the stick. In this fight and in this life. My first act as Alpha is to abolish all of the Old Laws."

Cheers fill the room except for a smell sect. "Any of you who cannot accept that, you are free to leave the pack now. In fact, I insist you do."

"Blasphemy!" someone hollers.

"What happened just now is blasphemy." I shake my head. "My second act as Alpha is to honor Bo. We will have a memorial for him. We will remember him. We will fight for people like him. We will heal generational wounds."

More cheers dance around me and I feel a warm hand slip in mine. Nette.

"And my third and final act for the night." I lift Nette's hand up in the air with mine. "I declare Nette my mate. She is mine. And I am hers."

"And," she whispers into the mic before raising her voice a bit, "I am both a member of the Midnight Shadows Pack and the Lone City Wanderers. I will officially be acting as a liaison between the two packs. And I promise, we will always remember my brother Bo. We will always fight for what is right."

"Exactly." I breathe. "Now as you can see, I've had a hard night and I need to get this stomach wound tended to." *And my soul...*

When we leave the arena and make our way home, I try to form the words to tell Nette how sorry I am. How do you say sorry I accidentally killed your twin brother who hated you and you never got a chance to know? I start to say it, the words, but tears take over.

"I must not look like much of a man to you right now," I mutter.

"Noah Kahan. You hush this instance with your internalized toxic masculinity, okay? Cry. Cry all you need. I want to cry with you, but to be honest, I am relieved. I am relieved that you are okay. I am happy he is gone. But you knew him. I didn't, Noah. In all reality, he was more of your brother once than he ever was or ever would be mine."

"I never wanted to hurt him. Or anyone. Not like this." I sob.

"I know. I know, Noah." She hugs me tight. "I am sorry this happened. I am so so sorry."

"I just want to go home."

"We are babe."

I realize now the car is moving. We are in a car. My mother and father sit across from us. A driver is taking us to our destination.

"I'm proud of you son," my father says. I tilt my head, noticing a strange yellow tint around his eyes. In his eyes, too. I've been so caught up in myself, my hatred with my family, my romance with Nette, and training for this stupid fight and overthrowing my parents polices that I didn't notice.

"Dad, you're sick."

My mother gasps. "I told you not to tell him!"

"I didn't!" Nette snaps, squeezing my hand.

"You knew?" I spin around to look Nette in the eyes. It's something I would once be so angry over, but now? Life — and death — has a much different place in my heart and mind now.

"It wasn't my secret to tell," Nette answers.

"We'll talk about this later," I say, squeezing her hand reassuringly. "Dad, how much longer do you have?"

"Straight to the point there, son!" He laughs. "I have long enough to see your mating ceremony. Beyond that, I'm not sure."

CHAPTER EIGHT

NETTE

I wrap Noah in my arms, kissing away his nightmares when I can, but stepping back when I can't. When kisses don't ease a pain so deep, I can't understand. I spend my days rushing to plan a mating ceremony. My mother and brothers and the entire Lone City pack join forces with Noah's mother to help bring my dream wedding to life.

I knew little about mating ceremonies, but Mrs. Kahan was quick to fill me in on the details.

"Don't worry. Nothing archaic when it comes to love."

"I'm glad to hear that! And glad Noah's abolishing those crazy laws."

"Me too." She sighs. "You must think I am a terrible person. A terrible mother."

"No," I reply quickly. Too quickly.

"You know how people say you don't know you're living in a burning house. I didn't know, Nette. This," she says and waves her hand around as I get fitted for my ceremony dress. "All of this was normal to me. The money. The wealth. The crazy rituals. You met Robbie... I guess now is a good time to tell you he's your uncle."

"What?" I gasp. "He's so..."

"Normal?" she laughs.

"I was mated to Noah's dad at a young age. My family always rejected things the way you do. But I didn't want to be like them. I saw nothing wrong with embracing who we are. Power corrupts, Nette. I guess what I am saying is, I'm glad you and Noah are taking over."

"And warning me," I respond, smiling.

"Don't let it corrupt you," she answers, matching my smile.

"Never," I promise.

One good thing about having a big family and pack —
now two big families — is I didn't have to do a single
ounce of planning. I just had to show up. With Noah's
father's growing illness, the liver failure giving him mere
weeks left to live, we almost have to have the ceremony in
the hospital. Shifters are strong. Their bodies heal. We live
longer. But we do succumb to illness after time. We are
subject to the same cruelties of the world as humans are.

My mom holds my arm as she leads me down an aisle of
sorts. Lone City pack members on one side and Midnight
Shadows pack on the other. Each looking at me like a
beacon of hope, and it humbles me deeply. My mother's
body shakes, and I am reminded of her own health scare
and the frailty of life.

In my hand she places a deep purple ribbon, an impor-
tant piece of the mating ceremony. Noah holds a white
ribbon. Together, we wrap the ribbon around our own
wrists and start wrapping it around each other as each pack
sings a mating hymn. Once we are bound, Noah beholds

my eyes. "I take thee, Nette, as my mate in this life and the next."

"I take thee, Noah, as my mate in this life and the next."

"Together," we say in unison, "Always. Forever."

"Now, I know it's a little hard with the ribbons keeping you two bound, but let's seal this ceremony with a kiss," the officiate declares.

We both chuckle. If they only knew! I pull my wrists tight to my chest, forcing Noah's body against mine. His lips take in my own and we kiss, a kiss of love and a promise for us and our people.

Together. Always. Forever.

As the celebration wraps around us, I keep an eye out for my birth parents. Both afraid and hopeful they might show up. It's silly, I know. I mean, why would they? My husband killed their child, my brother. And yet, I thought perhaps these changes, perhaps this experience, would enlighten them. I know this is common for children with abusive or absent parents, but damn... I thought I was over that. I guess some things never change.

"They won't be here," Mrs. Kahan says, handing me a glass of wine.

"Who?" I ask.

"Don't play dumb." She says, "We had them and their followers excommunicated. Noah did. He didn't want to stress you with it, but they won't be in town anymore. They've moved on."

I nod.

"Your mother over there is a lovely woman," she comments. "I'm glad you had the upbringing you did, even though I deeply regret the role my husband and I had in what happened to you."

"Thank you," I say.

Noah carries me over the threshold despite my protests. "Come on, it's not as if we haven't consummated this relationship already!"

"Oh, but not like this."

"What do you mean?"

"Oh, you have no idea what I have in store for you tonight, Mrs. Kahan."

I giggle, kicking my feet.

"I can't wait to take this dress off."

"Don't you dare rip this one!" I point my fingers at him. "This is my wedding dress, okay?"

"Yeah, yeah."

I expect him to toss me on his bed, but instead, Noan lays me down gently. No switches to secret chambers. Just him and me. He starts by kissing me, deep, hard, slow. Only coming up for air and to whisper his promises of love. A love I never thought I'd find, least of all, here, with a man who I thought was a monster — a rich monster. I could laugh at the irony of it all. Instead, I bask in each attentive kiss, each moment that I know is precious beyond reason. Noah nibbles my ears and moves his kisses back to my shoulders, my hands, fingers, before reaching his hands up my dress. The skirts are so long; he grows frustrated. "What is this dress made of?" He flails his arms.

"Allow me." I stand up and guide him to unzip the dress.

It falls to the floor to reveal a delicate, lacy number I picked out just for tonight.

"Damn," he says, praising me with his eyes. "You're perfect."

"You're not too bad yourself."

"Well, I hate to disappoint you," he says, unbuttoning his shirt and removing his pants. "I don't have any lingerie under these."

"It'll do," I reply with a wink.

His laugh sends me into a fit of giggles as he lifts me up, my legs wrapping around his waist. "Shh," he whispers, his hands sliding between my thighs, finding my clit.

"Ah," I moan.

"I see you're eager to consummate this mating marriage now, hm?"

"Mhm," I moan in response.

He places me back on his bed — our bed — and I reach for his hard cock, guiding him to me. He slides inside, and my body quivers along with his. Each stroke is filled with promises of love. For a second, I glance over at the chamber beside us. "Don't worry, love. We'll still play rough. Just not tonight. Tonight, I am going to love you down, every inch of you."

My hips respond in eager agreement. With each slow thrust, he deepens himself inside of me. Our bodies pick up our rhythm, our hands clasped, and even our souls melt into each other.

"Fuck," I cry out. "Noah, I'm so close," I plead. All the slow and sensual love making dissipates as my body rocks relentlessly against his and he follows suit.

"Nette," he moans, and it's enough to send shivers throughout my body. We cry out each other's names. I can feel myself tighten around his cock, both of us feverishly slamming against each other until we reach our orgasmic goal together.

"That was pretty fuckin' outstanding, if I do say so myself," Noah whispers.

"It was sweet," I whisper, a wicked smile on my face as I reach over and hit the switch.

"Woah," Noah teases. "I guess I can't compare to the pleasure chamber."

"Oh, you can. I'm just ready for more." I wink, standing up, dripping with need. I pull out my favorite clit sucker chains, and a whip. "We've had a rough few weeks. It's time to burn off some steam."

"You can say that again!" Noah jumps up and grabs the handcuffs. "Me or you?"

"You," I say, licking my lips.

He slaps them on me.

I bite my lip. "What are you doing?"

"You think I'm 'sweet', huh?" he teases, before pushing me back onto the bed and handcuffing me to the bedposts. With the clit sucker toy in hand, he lets the toy tend to me there while his mouth takes in my breasts, sucking my nipples. I get closer and closer when he stops sucking me. He reaches for the whip, and it crashes against my skin in the most delightful way as the toy continues its work.

His fingers explore me and each time I get closer, he whips me again, and I moan out in pleasure and pain. My hips are grinding in the air when he pulls away. I whimper, frustrated.

He tosses the toy and the whip aside before taking me in his mouth. "Fuck, Noah."

There isn't a toy in the world that could compare to the touch of this man — his lips, his skin — because it's him. He is mine. I am his. My hips grind against his tongue, always so close to coming before he stops yet again.

"Dammit, Noah! Is this any way to treat your wife?" I whine, my hips grind at the air, his dick hovering above me now. Hard and ready again. Lesson learned: I will never call Noah sweet again. Not if I want to come before the night ends.

"Oh, but it is," he purrs in my ear as he enters me once again. Just like that, all gentleness is out the window, as he grinds against me with a fury and passion that makes my body wake with need. "Yes, yes, yes!" I call out.

His nails dig into me, and I bite his shoulder. "Fuck, Nette," he moans. "I'm so close."

Tempted to stop and give him a taste of his own medicine, I am too consumed by the pleasure as I rock against him, our bodies once again our own erotic melody, reaching a crescendo as shivers wash over each of us in a climax that leaves us both weak and shaking.

"I love you, Nette," Noah whispers, his voice shaky.

"I love you too."

"It's me and you now," he says.

"Together," I continue.

"Always," he adds.

"Forever," I finish.

Who knew such a forbidden fruit could lead to such an endless, pleasurable delight?

EPILOGUE

NOAH

One Year Later

It's been one year since I married the love of my life. One year since I lost my best friend. One year since my father passed. And one year since I found out I was going to be a dad. In my arms, I hold the most beautiful baby that has graced this earth, let alone this pack. He was a surprise to us both — we had no idea how far along Nette was, let alone that she was pregnant. Now four months old, baby Bo is ready to take on the baby world. At least, that's what he thinks!

He has no idea the name he bears once was a great source of trauma for both me and his mom, but we both vowed to honor Bo. His uncle.

It's Nette's first day back at MidnightZ. Her first day as CEO. And my first official day being a "retired" man.

"Well, little Bo, what are we gonna do while mama's at work, huh?"

"I think you guys should work to overthrow anything that gets in your way." Nette tosses me a binky. "We've really come a long way, huh?"

I laugh. "I was just thinking that."

"Bo's initiation is next week," Nette says. "I was thinking maybe you could go visit Helping Hands. Show him off for a bit. I'll be home early today."

"You're stalling Nette." I say gently.

"I know, but he's only four months old! Should I really be going back to work?"

"You're only going back for less than part-time. My mother will be filling in still. You deserve a little break."

"I do," she says firmly. "And he has you. And we're shifters."

"We're shifters *and* we're Kahan's. We are strong. Go have fun. Trust me, today is going to be less work, and well, a little birdy told me it's more of a girl's day out."

"Noah!"

"With both my mom and your mom, so go. Shoo!"

"We have a crazy life, you know that, right?"

"I do."

And I wouldn't have it any other way.

Acknowledgements

A special "Thank You" to all of you who take the time to read my work.

With Love

Phoenix Skyy

Also By

Phoenix Skyy

Diva Crazy in Love

Because of You

Forbidden Series (1 - 3)

Also By

Mind Flow Publishing

The Mary B Chronicles (1- 4)

The Freedom in the Cage Series (1 - 4)

Finding Kate

A Chance at Love

Split Decision

Sophie's Pack

Mental Interlude

Spoken From the Heart

Simple Complexity

Falling in Love With Poetry

Charisma's Homecoming

www.ingramcontent.com/pod-product-compliance
Lightning Source LLC
Chambersburg PA
CBHW051812050726
47598CB00006B/2529